The Enchanted Horse

Collins
RED
STORYBOOK

Magdalen Nabb

The
Enchanted
Horse

Illustrated by Julek Heller

CollinsChildren'sBooks
An imprint of HarperCollins*Publishers*

This book is dedicated to
Maestro Nino Di Fazio
with admiration for his
boundless knowledge of horses.

First published in Great Britain by
CollinsChildren'sBooks 1992

CollinsChildren'sBooks is a division of
HarperCollins*Publishers* Ltd,
77-85 Fulham Palace Road,
Hammersmith, London W6 8JB

The HarperCollins website address is
www.fireandwater.com

19 21 23 25 24 22 20

Text copyright © Magdalen Nabb 1992
Illustrations copyright © Julek Heller 1992

The author and illustrator assert the moral right to be
identified as the author and illustrator of the work.

ISBN 0 00 674721 3

Printed and bound in Great Britain by
Omnia Books Ltd, Glasgow

★ ONE ★

It was Christmas Eve, and the afternoon had frozen as hard and milky as a pearl. The sun was as thin and pale as a disc of ice in a sky as white as the snowy ground.

Irina walked in front of her mother and father along the lane that led across the fields to the village. She was dressed in a sheepskin coat and boots and mittens and a sheepskin hat. Her long fair plait hung down behind her. The cold pinched her thin cheeks, and the trees that grew on each side of the lane poked their black fingers through the freezing fog as if they were trying to clutch at her as she went by.

Even before they reached the first houses at the edge of the village, Irina heard the faint sound of a band playing Christmas carols. But she didn't look up and smile or turn to say "Listen!" to her mother and father. She only walked quietly on, looking down at her thick boots as they trod the hardened snow. Irina didn't like Christmas.

When they reached the village, all the shop windows were already lit, making haloes of light in the fog. The snow-covered square where the band was playing round the Christmas tree was hung around with coloured bulbs. But Irina and her parents didn't stop to listen to the carols because they had so much to do. They lived on a farm and at Christmas everyone wants more cream and eggs and milk, and besides, they had to be back home in time to feed the animals. So her father stopped to talk to the dairyman at the corner and Irina went ahead with her mother to help with the shopping.

They went to the baker's to buy bread and flour and had to wait in a long queue. At the front of the queue a girl who was smaller than Irina reached up and pointed at the cakes and little pies sprinkled with icing sugar.

"And some of those," she shouted, "for Grandma! And the big cake! Grandpa likes cakes! The big cake!"

Irina watched her and listened to every

word, but when it was her mother's turn she didn't ask for anything. She was thin and never had much appetite and there was no Grandpa or Grandma coming for Christmas dinner.

They went to the greengrocer's and waited in the long queue. A fat little boy with a red scarf wound round and round his neck was quarrelling with his older sister.

"I like *dates* best!" he protested.

"No you don't," his sister said, "you only like the box with the picture on it, and we're going to buy figs and nuts and tangerines, so there." And their mother winked at the greengrocer's wife and bought figs and nuts and tangerines and dates.

Irina watched them and listened to every word, but when it was her mother's turn she didn't ask for anything. She had no brothers or sisters to quarrel with.

The band in the square began to play "O come, all ye faithful" and the fat little boy in the red scarf and his sister joined in the singing as they went out.

It was getting dark, and the coloured lights twinkled brighter now against the shadowy snow. On the corner outside the greengrocer's shop a fat lady with a long apron and thick gloves was selling

Christmas trees. A thin boy, taller than Irina, was choosing one with his father. "This one! No, this one, no, that one, *that* one, it's the biggest!" And his father laughed and said, "And how do you think we'll get it home?" But he bought it, even so, and the fat lady wound some thick string round it to help them carry it. Irina watched and listened but she didn't ask for anything. Years ago her mother had said, "You're too old now to be bothering about a Christmas tree. It's a waste of money. You can choose a nice present instead."

So they walked past the Christmas trees and crossed to the other side of the square. There was a toy shop there, and next to that a gloomy junk shop with a bunch of dusty mistletoe hanging in the window, and next to that a shop that sold pretty frocks with full velvet skirts. Irina stood beside her mother and stared at the shop windows with bright eyes but she didn't ask for anything. What was the use of a party frock when she lived so far from the village that she never went to a party? And what was the use of toys when there were no children near enough to play with?

"Have you thought what you'd like?" her mother asked. "You know we mustn't be long, we've a lot to do."

Irina tried to think. It's nice to be able to choose anything you want but it's nicer still when your present is a surprise. So she stared at the big dolls in boxes and then at the dresses and then at the tinsel and the silver bells decorating the window. She wanted to choose something that would please her mother. Then she remembered the fat little boy and his cheerful red scarf and so as not to keep her mother waiting and make her angry she said, "I like the red velvet frock . . ."

"And where do you think you'll go in it?" said her mother impatiently.

"I don't know . . ." It's hard to please your mother when you don't know exactly what she wants you to say. Then she turned and saw her father coming.

"Well?" he said, "Have you finished shopping? It's about time we were getting back."

"Irina hasn't chosen her present," said her mother crossly. "And to look at her face you'd think it was a punishment instead of a treat."

Irina wanted to say, "I don't want anything. I'm not asking for anything. I'd rather go home." But she didn't dare.

Then her father said, "Come on, let's have a look in that toy shop. There must be something you'd like."

"She's spoilt, that's what she is," her mother said. "She doesn't know what it means to want for anything."

The band in the square was playing "Silent Night" very quietly. The sadness of the music, the growing darkness, and the cheerfulness of all the other families made Irina want to cry.

"I don't want anything," she said to herself fiercely, "I don't—" But just as they were coming to the toy shop she stopped.

"Come on," said her father, "you're not going to find anything there."

But Irina didn't move. She was staring in through the window of the junk shop, trying to make something out in the gloom.

"Irina!" said her mother. "For goodness' sake, we have to get home."

But Irina, always so quiet and obedient, for once took no notice.

"The horse . . ." she said, "look at the poor horse."

"What horse?" said her father.

"I can't see any horse," said her mother. And they both peered into the gloomy junk shop. Beneath a jumble of dusty broken

furniture they could just make out the head and tattered mane of what was probably a rocking horse.

"I see it now," her father said, "Well, come on, let's get on. You don't want that old thing for Christmas."

"I should hope not," her mother said. "It looks filthy."

But Irina stared up at them bright-eyed, and the tears that had started with the sad carol and the growing darkness and the cheerfulness of all the other families spilled over and ran down her cheeks.

"It's being crushed," she cried. "It's lonely and frightened and being crushed under all those things!" And before her parents could stop her, she had run inside the shop and all they could do was to follow her.

★ TWO ★

Once inside, Irina stood still, wondering what to do. She'd never seen such confusion in a shop before. It didn't really look like a shop at all, more like the untidiest house in the world. The piles of old furniture reached right up to the ceiling and it was difficult to pass between them. There were ornaments, too, and brass buckets and lampstands and old stoves and typewriters and objects you couldn't tell the use of, and everything was thickly coated with dust, including the one bare light bulb which left most of the room in shadow.

"What can I do for you?" asked a voice in the gloom.

Irina looked about but she could see no one. She felt frightened, but she stood where she was and waited.

"Anyone at home?" said her father's voice behind her.

A voice chuckled. "I am," it said, "if you want to call this home. Past the big dresser on your left."

Irina looked round. At first she could make nothing out but then she noticed a huge armchair with carvings on it as big as a throne, and the profile of a man's head just visible.

"See me now?" But the head didn't turn and the eyes were shut. "I suppose it's getting dark, but I can't see and I don't know why I should pay out good money so that others can see. There's nothing much worth looking at, though I make a living after a fashion. What was it you wanted?"

"The rocking horse," Irina said, as loudly as she dared, and she went closer to the huge carved chair. The man seated there was almost as small and slight as herself, and his closed eyes were sunk in his white face so that he seemed to have no eyes at all. He wore a black overall and his pale hands rested on his knees as quietly as mice.

"Irina . . . !" protested her mother in an angry whisper. Irina stood where she was, her fists clenched in fear and determination.

"She saw the horse in the window . . ."

Irina's father began, but the blind man took no notice of him.

"What's your name?" he asked, his face lifted towards Irina.

"Irina."

"Irina," he whispered. "Come closer to me."

Irina was frightened of the blind man, but she had to rescue the horse. She went closer. The blind man lifted his mouse-like hands and touched her face, feeling her eyes, her thin cheeks, her mouth and her chin in turn.

"Irina," he said again, and he patted her face gently. "You're a very sad little girl. Why don't you play and be happy?"

"Because there's nobody to play with," Irina said.

"And that's why you want Bella? To play with?"

At first, Irina didn't answer because she didn't know who Bella was, but then she thought and said, "Is Bella the name of the horse in the window?"

"That's right," said the blind man.

"Then I don't want her to play with," Irina said boldly. "I want to look after her because she's dirty and lonely and crushed under all those heavy things in your window."

"In that case," said the blind man, "you'd better take her home with you."

Irina stood still and waited, wondering if her mother would say she couldn't, but nobody spoke until the blind man said, "Would you like to know why I call her Bella?"

"Yes," said Irina. "Did she belong to another girl who called her that?"

"I don't rightly know," the blind man said, "who she belonged to, but I'll tell you her story, such as it is. Do you remember a wicked farmer who used to live hereabouts who was known as Black Jack?"

"No," said Irina, "I don't."

"Well, well," said the blind man, "you're very young and it was all before your time."

"I remember him," said Irina's father, coming closer. "He kept horses."

"He did," said the blind man. "And the most beautiful one of all was named Bella because Bella means beautiful. But he was an evil man and treated his animals badly, very badly. They never got more than a handful of oats a day, barely enough to keep them alive, and Bella, who was as finely bred and elegant as a racehorse, was forced to pull him around in that dirty old cart of his. They say he whipped her until she bled. No one knew where he got her, but some said he captured her himself from a wild herd that sometimes passes by this way."

"And what happened to her?" Irina asked.

"I don't know," the blind man said. "But I can tell you what happened to Black Jack. He died."

"I remember," said Irina's father. "I went to the auction when his farm was sold. My old father was still alive then and he kept a pony and trap himself. It was he who talked me into going, but there was little enough worth buying and the horses were only fit for the knacker's yard."

"Even Bella?" asked Irina.

"Bella wasn't there," the blind man said, "Bella wasn't there. I asked about and I spoke to the auctioneer himself but there was no horse of that description on his list. Poor creature. Poor beautiful creature . . ."

The blind man fell silent with his thoughts as if he'd forgotten there was anyone there.

"Was she dead, then . . . ?" whispered Irina after a while.

"I bought all that stuff in the window from Black Jack's place," the blind man said, without giving her an answer, "and there it's been ever since, including the horse."

"Now what would Black Jack have wanted a rocking horse for?" wondered Irina's father. "He had neither wife nor child."

"But that's just it," said the blind man very softly, just as if he were talking to himself. "It's not a rocking horse."

Then he spoke more loudly, turning his face up towards Irina's father's voice.

"Take the horse home for your little Irina," he said. "If it will make her happy I don't want anything for it. Only perhaps you'll have to come for it another day when the boy who helps me is here. You understand. I can't move all that stuff to get at it."

"That's very nice of you," said Irina's father. "We'll call another time."

He took Irina by the shoulder, but Irina, who never asked for anything, cried, "Please! Please can we wait in case he comes?" And she touched the blind man's arm, no longer afraid of him. "*Please* let us wait! You can tell us more stories about Bella."

"Come on, now," said her father, and he led her to the door. "You know we have to get home."

"And don't imagine we're coming back," warned her mother as they went. "That

filthy thing must be a mass of woodworm
and it's not coming into the house."

Outside on the snowy pavement Irina
began to cry. The band was still playing
under the Christmas tree and the people had
finished their shopping and were starting for
home loaded with parcels and calling to each
other under the winking lights.

"Merry Christmas! Merry Christmas to
you!"

Before her parents could take her away,
Irina turned her tearful face for a last look
at Bella's poor head, crushed under all that
junk, and then from inside the shop the
blind man's voice called out, "Stop!"

It was as if he had given an order that had
to be obeyed. Irina's parents hesitated and
looked at each other.

"Come back a moment, if you will."

Irina's father shrugged. "I suppose we'd
better see what the poor old chap wants."

They went back inside the gloomy shop,
and Irina ran straight to the blind man's
chair. He was sitting just as they'd left him,
with his hands resting quietly on his knees.

"I never mistake a footstep," he said.
"When you can't see you learn to recognize
people in other ways." Then he lifted his
face up and called, "Hurry up, now! We

have customers waiting!"

Irina turned round, and saw a tall cheerful boy come in from behind where her parents stood watching.

"I came to wish you Merry Christmas, Grandad!"

The grinning boy spoke at the top of his voice as though the man were deaf rather than blind.

"And just as well you did," said the blind man, "there's a job for you to do. This is Irina, and she wants to take Bella home with her, so you'll have to get her out from under all that stuff in the window."

"Right you are, Grandad!" said the boy.

"I don't think . . ." began Irina's mother, but the boy had already climbed into the window and was heaving the broken furniture about. "I'll have her out of here in two minutes!"

"Is he your grandson?" asked Irina shyly.

"No," said the blind man, "but that's what he likes to call me."

"I haven't got a grandad," Irina said, and she stared at the blind man, wishing he were her grandad, because he could make her parents do what he told them.

"Here you are!" said the boy, and he set Bella down on the floor by Irina. She touched the dirty tangled mane timidly.

"Your father will carry her home for you," the blind man said. "She's too heavy for you."

And sure enough, without a word of protest, Irina's father came and picked up Bella.

"She's a fair weight," he said, "but I'll manage."

"I'll help you," Irina said.

"You help your mother carry the shopping," said her father. Irina followed him to the door, holding her breath because she could hardly believe they were really taking Bella away. But once they were outside she remembered something and ran back.

"Thank you," she said to the blind man. "And thank you for getting Bella out for me," she said to the cheerful boy who was perched on the arm of the huge chair, swinging his long legs.

"Goodbye, Irina, and Merry Christmas," said the old man, and he lifted his small white hands towards her. She went closer, understanding now that he needed to touch her because he couldn't see her. "Be happy," he said gently and patted her cheek.

"I will be happy," Irina promised, "and I'll look after Bella – and can I . . . can

I come back and see you one day?" She would have liked to ask him if she could call him Grandad, like the boy, but she didn't dare.

"Come whenever you like," said the blind man, "I'm always here."

"Merry Christmas!" she whispered, her eyes shining, and she ran outside.

★ THREE ★

All the long way home, Irina's mother had a lot to say about moths and woodworm and dirt not coming into her clean house, but Irina hardly heard her she was so happy, and by the time they reached the farm it had been settled that Bella should be put in the old barn which in any case was already half full of junk, where she would dirty nothing and be in nobody's way.

"Can we put straw down for her?" Irina asked as Bella was carried in.

"You can do as you like," her father said. "But you'd better change into your old clothes first, or you'll have your mother after you." And he stood Bella in a corner of the barn just inside the door.

"Let me just look at her first," said Irina. "I won't touch her, I just want to look."

They both looked. It was a sorry sight. There was no telling what colour the horse was meant to be because she was so thickly coated with dirt. Her mane and tail seemed to be of real horsehair, matted, tangled and filthy. It was difficult to tell just what she was made of but it was true, as the blind man had said, that she wasn't a rocking horse. She stood square on her four hooves, and there was nothing to suggest that she had ever had rockers. Her head drooped a little and her eyes under the tattered fringe were squeezed almost shut, as though she were crying.

"Poor creature . . ." whispered Irina, imitating the blind man's words.

"Come on, we've got work to do," her father said, slapping the dust from his hands and coat. "Get changed and start collecting the eggs. We're late with the milking."

Irina was used to working hard on the farm, and since there were no children around to play with she never minded it. But that evening she worked twice as fast as usual so that she would have time to visit Bella before supper.

She ran so fast with the heavy baskets of eggs that if she didn't break any it was only because she was lucky not to slip on the icy stones of the farmyard, and it was a wonder that she didn't give the hens calf nuts to eat by mistake.

Even so, by the time she had finished all her jobs there was only time to lay down some fresh straw for Bella before her mother called.

"Irina! Come and lay the table, supper's ready!"

"I have to go in," Irina whispered to Bella, stroking the poor tangled head. "But tomorrow I'll come and see you before we go to church and afterwards I'll brush and comb you and talk to you so you won't be lonely."

"Irina!"

She turned off the light and went into the house.

Because there was some extra cooking and baking to help with for next day, it was late when Irina went up to bed. In her nightdress, she sat on the bed and parcelled up the little presents she had made at school for her mother and father. She was so happy that they had let her have Bella that she would have liked to give them something bigger and better, but there was nothing she could do about it now. Perhaps she could think of an extra job to do tomorrow to help her father. And if she said she was hungry and ate more than usual her mother would be pleased. She always looked worried and cross when Irina left food on her plate.

When the parcels were tied and ready, Irina put them on the chair by the bed. But she felt too excited to go to sleep, and went to look out of her window where one of the apple trees that grew in the yard almost touched the panes with its bare branches. It was too dark to see the old barn properly, but Irina stood there a long time with her head pressed against the glass, thinking of Bella and listening to faint noises of the cold night.

And in the darkness of the barn with the clean straw spread around her, Bella stood with her head lowered and her eyes half closed as though she, too, were listening.

★ FOUR ★

Irina was the first to wake on Christmas morning. Dawn hadn't broken, and the house was hushed and dark. She wrapped herself up warmly and tiptoed down the stairs and out across the icy yard to the old barn.

"Bella!" she called softly, as she pulled the big door open and switched on the light, "Bella! It's Christmas . . ."

Her eyes shone with pleasure as she approached the horse and reached out to touch its stiff ears and tangled mane.

"Don't be sad," she said gently, "you won't be lonely any more now because I'll come every day and talk to you and brush you and give you clean straw."

She knelt beside Bella and lifted the matted fringe from her sad eyes.

"I'll find you an old blanket, too, if I can, because the nights are so cold. And then in the spring I'll take you outside in the meadow where there'll be grass and flowers and a stream for you to drink from. Will you like it? Will you, Bella?"

She would have liked to put her arms round Bella's neck and hug her tight to make her sadness go away, but she was still shy of her. Instead she promised: "After Christmas dinner I'll be able to stay with you all afternoon and I'll wash and comb you so you'll look beautiful."

Then she got to her feet and tiptoed to the door. Before she switched the light off she said: "Merry Christmas, Bella."

Out in the yard it was still dark. Irina mixed some mash ready for the hens as a surprise for her father. Then she washed her hands in the dairy and pulled off her boots to go in and lay the table for breakfast as a surprise for her mother. They were surprised, but not because she'd done the extra work. Her father gave her a pat on the head and said, "Well! You look as bright and cheery as a robin this morning. What's come over you?"

Her mother, watching her eat her breakfast quickly, looked puzzled and said: "You've got an appetite all of a sudden. What's come over you?"

By the time they were ready to go to church, the day was bright and clear. The freezing fog had vanished in the night and the big winter sun made the icicles shine like glass and the snowy fields sparkle like Christmas glitter. All the way along the lane that led to the village Irina looked happily about her at the blue shadows on the snow, the few crinkly brown leaves and stalks poking out of the frozen ditch, and the darting black shapes of birds looking for berries, and she thought to herself, "I love Christmas!"

Inside the church it was dark after the dazzling snow, but the crib in the corner was lit by glimmering candles. After the mass Irina went and knelt there, looking at the still figures kneeling in the hay. The Baby in the manger held out his stiff arms towards her, and Irina wished she were alone so that she could explain all about Bella, but more and more people were queuing up behind her. She smiled at the donkey on his pile of straw and then dropped her coins into the box and lit a candle, liking the warm smell of the wax.

And after the cold tramp home there was

the warm smell of Christmas dinner.

"I'm hungry!" Irina said, and again her parents looked surprised but they didn't say anything.

After dinner her mother and father admired their little presents and then settled in their armchairs, their faces rosy with sleep after the long morning. Before their eyes were quite closed, Irina said, "Can I go out to the barn?

"Mmmm . . ." was all her mother said, and her father gave a little startled grunt as if wondering who had spoken. So Irina wrapped herself up and went out.

She ran first to the barn to stroke Bella and then she began fetching and carrying things across the yard. She fetched two heavy buckets of warm water, a cake of soap, an old sponge from under the sink in the dairy and two old towels that hung behind the door of the cowshed. Then she crept back into the house and went upstairs to get her own comb. She needed a brush too but she didn't dare take her own hairbrush in case it got spoiled and her mother found out. As long as she didn't break the comb she could wash it afterwards and no one would know. Then she was ready to start work.

First, she washed Bella's mane and tail, being as careful as she could not to let the soapy water get into the horse's eyes. She washed and rinsed and washed and rinsed but the hair still felt coarse and greasy and she had to fetch two more buckets of clean warm water and do it all again.

"I think it's clean now," she said, "but I'll need more water for your coat and your feet." And off she went again with the buckets. But when she started to wash Bella's coat she got a surprise. She had thought that Bella would be made of painted wood like a rocking horse, but she wasn't.

"Your coat's real," she said, "just like your mane and tail . . ."

She soaped it all over very carefully and rinsed away the dirty suds with the sponge. It was a real coat all right, and though it was still wet it looked as if it would be quite a pale colour. Irina washed the horse's feet, and then used the last bucket of clean water to sponge her face and ears very gently. Then she rubbed her all over with the towels, and started work with her comb. She combed the tail first and then the mane, holding the long hair and starting from the ends the way she did with her own hair, because that way it didn't hurt. It took a long time.

"There," she said at last, "all finished."

Then she remembered something.

She remembered her grandfather. At least, she didn't remember him exactly because he had died when she was only a baby, but she remembered her father talking about him and how he had kept a pony and trap all his life. Irina went to the far end of the barn where her father kept what he called "Things that might come in useful" and her mother called "Junk that wants throwing out". She began to look at everything carefully. She didn't know exactly what she was looking for, but if her grandfather had kept a pony then there might just be something useful for Bella. She was right. It took her a long time and she bumped and scratched herself climbing over bits of old farm implements, and almost choked on the clouds of dust that flew up as she pulled at pieces of torn sacking. But right at the back in the corner, weighed down by what looked like part of a plough, she discovered a wooden trunk with a broken metal lock. The box was hemmed in by so many other things that she had no hope of getting it out, but she did manage to drag away the heavy piece of plough from the top and open it. It was impossible in the dark corner to see properly what the box contained, but Irina felt inside and pulled the things out. One by one she climbed out with them to where she could see.

"Bella! Look!" she cried, examining her treasure. "There's everything for you, even a blanket!" And there was.

The blanket was old and far too big for Bella, but still it would keep her warm. And there were combs and brushes and bits of harnesses and reins whose leather had rotted away. Irina didn't know the use of half the things, but she put everything in a tidy pile in the corner behind Bella except for the blanket.

The blanket she put carefully over Bella, who was still very wet. It was so big that she folded it double and even then it covered the horse completely from head to tail.

"It doesn't look very nice," Irina explained, "but we have to keep you warm."

She stroked Bella's nose, which was all that was visible under the heavy blanket, and said, "Now you can have a long long sleep until tomorrow."

When she came out of the barn the winter sun was setting, huge and red, and all the snow was lit with a pink light.

Irina thought, "It's almost the end of Christmas Day." But she didn't feel sad, she felt excited as if instead of the end of something it was the beginning of something. And it was.

★ FIVE ★

"Irina!" called her mother from the dairy. "Are you supposed to be helping or not? Irina!"

The sun glittered on the snow in the yard, but no answer came, and no Irina came either.

"Irina!" called her father like an echo, "Irina! Your mother's calling you!"

But still Irina didn't come.

The broken door of the big barn stood open and the morning sun beamed in low, its light glittering with reflections from the snow. Inside the door, Irina stood holding the old blanket, her face as bright as the sunshine as she gazed in astonishment at the result of her work. She had hoped, when she took off the blanket that morning, that Bella would look clean and pretty but she hadn't hoped for this.

Bella was beautiful. She stood there in the broad beam of sunlight and her coat was smooth and fine, the colour of the palest sand. Her mane and tail were as blonde as Irina's long hair, glowing with gold and silver lights picked out by the morning sun. She no longer looked sad, she looked so sleek and elegant that Irina felt all her shyness come back, and she felt afraid to touch such a beautiful creature. Very timidly, still clutching the blanket, she went closer, and she saw then that something was wrong. Bella was not perfect. Across her back there were marks, reddish marks like stripes. Irina forgot her shyness. She dropped the blanket and went closer still. Those marks were the marks of a whip!

"Oh no . . ." whispered Irina. She remembered the frightening story of Black Jack, who whipped and starved his horses. Had he been so cruel and stupid that he even whipped a horse that wasn't real and could do no work for him?

"Poor Bella." She knelt beside the horse and put her arms round its neck, feeling the thick silky mane against her cheek. "It must have hurt when I scrubbed and scrubbed at you but I didn't know. I couldn't see under all that dirt. And now I don't know what to do. I could fetch some ointment for you, the sort we use if the cows hurt themselves out in the pasture – but I don't know if real ointment will work on a pretend horse . . ."

"Irina! I won't tell you again!"

Irina scrambled to her feet.

"I have to go and help my mother – and I will bring some real ointment and try it."

She ran to the dairy and started working hard without a word, thinking all the time of Black Jack and his whip as though she were afraid he might come back to life.

"I don't know what's the matter with you," her mother said, after she'd told her to do something three times without getting an answer. "You look as though you're in a dream. There's no time for dreaming when there's work to be done."

Irina hardly heard her. All day she watched for the chance to get the ointment from the cowshed without anyone seeing. At last, when it was almost supper time, she managed it. She ran to the barn with the big jar hidden under her coat. The ointment was thick and had a strong smell. Very carefully she smoothed it over each of the angry red weals on Bella's back. Then she put her own clean handkerchief over the worst part. It wasn't really big enough but it would help to protect the sore parts from the rough heavy blanket. She tidied the straw around Bella's feet and gave her a little kiss on the nose that was as soft and smooth as velvet. Then she said Goodnight.

For three days Irina put ointment on Bella's sore back, and each time she had to sneak the jar out of the cowshed without anyone seeing her and sneak it back in afterwards. On the fourth day the marks were gone. On the fifth day she brought scissors and trimmed Bella's fringe so that it didn't fall in her eyes so much. Every morning and every evening she brushed Bella's sandy yellow coat and combed her silvery mane and tail, and on the sixth day, when Bella was quite perfect, she had an idea.

"I'll bring you some of the cow's hay," she said. "They won't mind." Her father would mind if he found out, she knew that. He'd let her have a bit of straw, but hay was much more expensive. Still, she would only take a little bit, and since Bella could only pretend to eat it she wouldn't ever have to take any more.

So that night, when Irina said Goodnight to her, Bella had clean straw around her feet, a thick blanket to keep her warm and a small heap of sweet-smelling hay in front of her.

Irina went to bed at nine o'clock. At first she couldn't get to sleep although she had worked hard and was tired. A terrible blizzard had begun during supper. The wind howled and whined in the chimneys and flung the branches of the

apple tree against her bedroom window
where snowflakes whirled and flew so
thickly that they made her dizzy as she
lay watching them. Irina liked the snow
when it fell softly, but the screaming wind
frightened her and made her think again of
Black Jack the evil farmer. Even though she
was warm and snug under her thick quilt,
she shivered at the noise of the blizzard and
hoped that Bella would be warm enough

under her blanket. And at last, thinking of Bella, her eyes closed and she fell asleep.

She slept heavily for a long time, and what it was that woke her she didn't know. One minute she was fast asleep, and the next minute she was sitting bolt upright in her bed, wide awake and staring at the window. It seemed to her that a sudden noise, like a door banging, had woken her, but now everything was silent. The blizzard had stopped, as blizzards do, as suddenly as it had begun, and now the full moon was shining in at her window, bright and silvery in a starry sky. Irina gazed at the moon, her body tense and her heart beating loud and fast. Something must have woken her but now it was all quiet, too quiet. The black boughs of the apple tree were still, and yet something out there was moving, she was sure of it. A soft swishing noise – there *was* something! Then a muffled pattering noise!

Irina jumped out of bed and ran to the window. She pressed her forehead to the cold glass and looked down, her heart beating so loudly that it hurt. Down in the yard the big door of the barn stood open, and a beautiful horse, its mane flowing like quicksilver in the moonlight, was trotting swiftly round in wide circles in the snow.

★ SIX ★

"Bella!" called Irina softly. The beautiful horse stopped and tossed up her head. Then she spun round on her hind legs and trotted towards the sound of Irina's voice. Right beneath the window she stopped again and looked up, her whole body quivering. She stretched her head forward towards the ground and started to paw at it with her front hoof, striking the icy stones and shaking her silvery mane.

"I'm coming!" cried Irina, and she ran out of her room and down the stairs, swift and silent in her bare feet.

"Bella!" As soon as she saw Irina the horse began trotting in circles again, her head turning this way and that as though she were looking for something. Suddenly, she stopped beside the stump of a tree where

48

Irina's father always chopped wood. She settled there, standing square on her four hooves, and turned her head towards Irina, waiting.

Irina understood at once. Without stopping to think of her bare feet and thin nightdress, without wondering whether she shouldn't feel afraid, she ran to the tree stump and climbed on to it and in a moment she was on Bella's back and holding the streaming silver mane. With a soft whinny of pleasure, Bella turned and cantered towards the farmyard gate. She checked and gathered herself and then leapt. Irina hardly felt the jump. It felt more like flying. Her cold bare feet clung to Bella's smooth warm sides, and her fingers entwined themselves in the thick mane, and they were off like the wind across the wide snowy fields.

The snow was so deep after the blizzard that Bella's hoof beats were almost silent, and the moon was so big and bright that they could see for miles and miles. On and on they went, flying over hedges, fences and ditches, speeding through copses where Irina had to rest her cheek on Bella's mane to avoid the snow-laden branches, then out again across the white fields in the moonlight. Irina didn't think to wonder where Bella was taking her. She didn't think of being frightened. She didn't think of being cold. She didn't think of anything. She felt the warmth of Bella's galloping body, the strong thick mane in her fingers, the ever-increasing speed that lifted her long hair and made it stream out behind like the horse's tail. More than anything else she felt happy.

At last, Bella began to turn in a wide circle. She jumped a low fence and galloped for home, and all too soon they were over the gate and back in the farmyard. Bella halted, and then walked quietly to the tree stump to let Irina slide down from her back. She was panting, and her breath was steamy in the night air. Irina got down from the tree stump and went to stroke Bella's neck. Bella lowered her head and turned to nuzzle Irina's hair with her warm velvety nose, then she trotted off into the barn and stood quietly in her corner on the straw. Irina hurried after her.

"I have to put your blanket on you. You're so hot with galloping and now you'll be cold." She picked up the heavy blanket but no matter how she tried she couldn't lift it on to Bella's back. She could only reach up to her shoulder. Bella turned

to look at her, with big, gentle eyes, waiting patiently. Irina didn't know what to do. She tried again but the blanket was so heavy and Bella was so tall that it was impossible.

"I can't reach you," she told Bella. "You were only small before and now I can't reach."

Bella must have understood, then. She began turning round and round in her corner, pawing and scraping at the straw beneath her feet. When it was smooth and flat she knelt down very carefully and then lowered her hind quarters. Irina covered her with the blanket and Bella at once sat up, straightened her front legs and sprang upright, shaking herself. Irina ran to fetch a bucket of water and some hay – "In case you get hungry and thirsty," she said, placing these in front of Bella. "Goodnight." She reached up to stroke Bella's cheek, but the horse didn't lower her head and nuzzle her as Irina would have liked. She stood very still and straight, looking very serious, and slowly raised her left front hoof.

"What is it, Bella? I don't understand. Have you hurt it?" Bella went on standing with her foot raised for a long time. Then, seeing that Irina did nothing, she put it down and lifted the right one, still looking straight ahead and waiting. She lifted each of her four feet in turn. Perhaps, in the end, she understood that Irina didn't know what to do, so she bent to nuzzle her as if to say Goodnight.

Irina ran into the house and climbed the stairs. As she crept past her parents' bedroom she heard her father snoring. She ran to her own room and jumped into bed, snuggling down under the quilt. She was so happy that she fell asleep at once to dream of riding over the snowy fields with Bella.

"Irina? Irina!"

Irina opened her eyes and sat up. It was morning and her mother was calling her.

"Irina! I've been calling you for the last half hour!"

But Irina didn't move at once. She was trying to remember something. Something had happened. She felt different today. Then she remembered her dream of riding over the snow. Could a dream make her feel so happy and so different? She got up and dressed quickly. The dream was still whirling around in her head, making her feel confused. She ran downstairs and through the kitchen towards the back door.

"Irina!" her mother said, "where do you think you're going? You're already too late to help me with the hens, and now breakfast's ready."

"I just want to go out for one minute, please—"

"Sit down," her mother said. "Your father's already in from milking."

Her father walked into the kitchen and Irina sat down at the table. They didn't usually talk much at breakfast. A lot of work had already been done, and a lot more was waiting to be done, and so they ate in a hurry. But this morning Irina's father had something to tell them.

"That was a fair blizzard we had last night," he began. "There are drifts as high as a man in some parts." He chewed in silence for a moment, then gulped at his drink, frowning. "It's a funny thing, but all over the yard there are prints in the fresh snow."

Irina's mother put down the plate she was about to carry away.

"Don't tell me a fox—"

"No. You don't need to start fretting about your hens. There's nothing missing, and besides, they weren't a fox's prints."

"What then?"

Irina stared silently at her plate as they talked, her heart beating faster and faster, her face growing redder and redder.

"A horse, I reckon."

It wasn't a dream. It *wasn't*.

"Are you sure?" her mother said. "I don't see how a horse could have got in with the five-barred gate shut."

"Jumped it," her father said, getting up to go out with a full steaming mug still in his hand. "There's a wild herd passes this way twice a year, but it's early days for them yet. The streams are all still frozen. There were some other prints as well, but I couldn't make them out."

"It was Bella!" said Irina, suddenly breaking her silence.

"And who's Bella?" asked her father, standing his mug on the end of the dresser near the door and sitting down to pull on his boots.

"My horse. She. . . last night I. . . ." Her voice tailed off and she looked down at her plate again, wishing she hadn't said anything.

"Irina, clear the table," her mother said.

"But it *was* Bella," Irina insisted quietly.

"You listen to me, young lady," said her mother sharply. "Making up stories at your age means telling lies. You're not a two year old. Clear that table. And I've had enough of you messing in that barn half the day when there's work to be done. If there's any more of it, I'll pitch that worm-eaten old thing out."

"Now, now," interrupted her father mildly, "leave her be. It's something for her to play with. She'll forget about it when school starts." And he went out.

Irina helped clear the table and wash the dishes in silence. And all the time she was thinking to herself, "It's not a lie. If they go in the barn, they'll see! They'll *see*. . ."

But first she had to see for herself. She had to escape from her mother's watchful eyes. It was a long time before she managed it, but at last she got out into the yard and ran to open the door of the old barn.

"Bella. . .?"

She was there in her corner, small and still, almost buried in the blanket that was far too big for her. Irina's heart was filled with confusion and disappointment. She knelt beside the little horse, and turned back the big blanket to stroke her mane. Then she saw that the hay was gone and the water bucket was empty.

★ SEVEN ★

Bella was real. Whatever happened to her in the daytime, at night she was real. Dreams don't eat hay and drink water. Dreams don't leave hoof prints in the snow.

Every night, Irina went to bed as early as she could and slept happily until Bella came to wake her, knowing that when the moon was high she would hear the noise of hooves striking on the icy stones in the yard. Then she would run to the window and see Bella waiting for her out in the white moonlit world of night.

They rode far and fast, as free as birds, and during their journeys Irina never spoke a word. She clung to Bella with her toes and fingers, her eyes bright and her hair streaming behind her as they flew across the snowy fields like the wind.

She never tried again to tell her parents the truth. She knew it would only make them angry. And yet she had to tell somebody – not just for the sake of telling, because Irina was an only child and used to keeping her secrets to herself, but because she was worried about something. Each night after their ride, when Bella trotted back into the barn, she continued to lift up each of her feet in turn, waiting. Irina had to ask someone what it meant.

Then she remembered the blind man. He knew all about Bella and he had said Irina could go back and see him whenever she wanted. Her chance came when school started. One day a week, Irina's mother came to school to meet her and they did some shopping. Irina waited until they were in a long queue in the grocer's which was only a step away from the blind man's junk shop.

"Can I go out and look in the shop windows?" Irina asked.

"If you like – but stay on this side of the square where I can find you."

"I will!" Irina ran as fast as she could and then paused at the gloomy entrance to the junk shop. Would the blind man recognize her footsteps and call out the way he did with that boy on Christmas Eve? No sound came from inside.

"Can I come in?" asked Irina timidly, taking a step forward.

"Of course you can," came the voice of the blind man.

Irina knocked the snow from her boots and went towards the big carved armchair. The blind man was sitting there just as before, as if he had never moved since Irina last saw him.

"And how is little Irina?" he asked.

"Did you recognize my steps?"

"No," said the blind man, "you haven't been to see me often enough for that, but I never forget a voice. And are you happy now with Bella?"

"Yes, I am," Irina said, and then she hesitated, wondering if he would believe her if she told the truth.

After a moment's silence the blind man said, "You might as well tell me, now you've come." Just as though, blind as he was, he could see into her thoughts. So Irina told him the truth about her night rides.

"So Bella *must* be a real horse," she said at the end. "And she's mine, all mine, and that's why I'm happy, only what am I to do about her feet? There's nobody else I can ask except you."

"Give me your hand," the blind man said, lifting his own pale, mouse-like hands towards her. Irina gave him her hand.

"What you say is not true," he said gravely.

"But she is real, she *is*!" protested Irina, tears of disappointment filling her eyes. "I thought you would understand. I thought you knew about Bella."

"Bella is God's creature," the blind man said sternly.

"You don't believe me!"

"Many people believe what you believe," the blind man said, "and all of them are unhappy just as you will be unhappy if you go on believing what is false." He lifted his hand to her cheek. "You're crying, but you'll shed bitter tears before long if you don't listen to what I tell you. Never say what is false. Never say that any creature on this earth is yours. Now, go behind my chair to where there's a big chest and take the parcel that's lying there. It's for you. You see, I was expecting you."

Irina went to the big chest, and took the parcel that was lying on its dusty surface.

"Thank you," she said, but she was still

crying tears of disappointment because he didn't believe her. She tried to dry her eyes on the back of her glove and had one last try.

"Couldn't a spell have been put on Bella to stop her being real, to save her from Black Jack so that he couldn't hurt her any more? Couldn't that be what happened?"

"There's a book in that parcel," the blind man said, without answering her. "Read it carefully. And if you want to go on being happy, remember my words. Never deceive yourself into believing something that isn't true."

Irina ran out of the junk shop and said to herself that she would never, *never* go there again. Grown-ups were all as bad and it was useless to tell them anything. It was better to talk just to Bella. Even if she couldn't answer, she always understood. And as soon as they got home she did talk to Bella for as long as she could before supper.

"I don't care any more if nobody believes me," she told Bella, stroking her mane. "From now on I'm only going to tell my secrets to you."

She quite forgot about the parcel until she was going up to bed. She saw it lying on the chair where she had dropped it when she came in, and though she hated the blind man now she couldn't help being curious about what was in it.

Upstairs, she settled down in bed and untied the string on the parcel. It was a book, as the blind man had said, and not a nice-looking book either, it was old and its hard red cover had faded to a greyish pink. Its spine was broken and some of the pages had come loose. One of these slipped out and fell from the bed to the floor, but not before Irina had noticed that there was a picture on it. A picture of a horse. She reached down to pick it up. The horse in the picture was standing with one foot raised, and a man was bending over the foot with what looked like a paintbrush in his hand. Quickly, Irina opened the book at its title page and read *Feeding, Grooming and Training Your Horse*.

Then the blind man had believed her, in spite of everything he'd said. He must have believed her if he gave her a book that would help her look after Bella! Irina wasted no time wondering why he should have behaved so strangely. She started to read the book as fast as she could. It had been written for adults, not for anyone as young as Irina, and there were many words in it that she couldn't understand. Even so, there were plenty of pictures to help her, and she recognized a lot of the things she had found in her grandfather's trunk.

Later that night, when they had ridden as far as they felt like riding over the snow and were back in the barn, Irina knew what she had to do when Bella stood patiently holding up her foot. At least, she thought she did. She was ready with all the right implements from the pile of her grandfather's things in the corner, and she knew she had to scrape the stones and dirt from under Bella's hoof and wipe it clean and then paint hoof grease on it with a brush. But learning practical things from a book by yourself is not the best way of learning, and it was lucky for Irina that she had a teacher on hand: Bella. Bella might not know how to speak, but she knew just what had to be done and how it should be done. She gave Irina her left front foot and turned to watch her as she worked, nuzzling her back every so often to encourage her. Irina's first attempt was slow, but at last she straightened up and said, "There, that's one finished." She went round to Bella's right and waited for the right foot to be offered her but nothing happened.

"You have to give me your right foot now, Bella."

Bella stood still. What could be wrong? Every night Bella had offered her feet one by one, first at the front, then at the back.

"Bella?" Irina looked up at her, stroking her neck. "What is it?" But Bella only stood there, tall and pale and elegant, gazing straight ahead, blinking her big soft eyes. At last, Irina remembered that the pictures in the book showed the man always working from the horse's left side. She went back to where she had stood before and Bella at once lifted her right foot and passed it to her behind the left. Irina got to work again, and Bella turned and nuzzled her back to tell her she was doing it right. When all four hooves were clean and shiny, Bella knelt to have her blanket put on and Irina brought her hay and water and said Goodnight.

Just before she fell asleep in her warm bed, Irina thought, "Perhaps one day, when she feels well and safe again, Bella will be a real horse all the time."

And she was right.

★ EIGHT ★

There was a time, before she had Bella, when Irina always walked sadly home after school, knowing that all the other children would be running in and out of each other's houses in the village or perhaps skating on the big pond nearby. Irina had never been allowed to stay and play. The winters were so long, and darkness came down so quickly, that her mother had always made her come straight home. And so she had always gone sadly on her way, looking back sometimes when she heard the others calling to each other and laughing.

But now it was different. Irina was always first out of the school gate, her long plait bobbing and swinging as she ran towards the long lane that led towards home and Bella. She would arrive red-cheeked and out of breath, and hurry straight into the big barn, calling, "Bella! I'm home!"

Then she would brush Bella's coat and comb her mane and chatter to her about everything that had happened at school that day, sure that the little horse was listening to every word. Then, at night, when Bella was her real tall beautiful self, they would ride.

One night, when the ice was creaking on the roofs and the streams bubbling under the snow, Bella galloped much farther away than usual. Instead of making a big circle and then heading for home, she went on and on, faster and faster over the flat snowy fields towards the horizon. Then, very suddenly, she stopped dead, her head lifted and her whole body tense and quivering.

"What is it?" Irina asked. "Bella, what is it?"

Bella remained rigid, her ears pricked. Had she heard something? Smelt something? Irina clung to Bella's quivering body and looked about her at the miles of snowy fields, the velvety sky dotted thickly with stars, the silver moon. She could see no danger. Then she wondered if they were near Black Jack's old farm. She had no idea where it was but then, they had come so far that she didn't recognize anything.

"Bella," she whispered, shivering and clutching tighter at the long mane, "let's go home. I'm frightened."

But Bella didn't hear or turn to nuzzle Irina's toes. She didn't move and Irina could feel the horse's great heart beating so fast and loudly that it seemed as if it must burst. Still Bella stared, her eyes fixed on the horizon. She whinnied, almost under her breath, then she relaxed. Whatever she had heard or smelt was gone. She turned her head to nuzzle Irina's cold toes with her warm nose and then took off at a gallop for home.

The next night the same thing happened, but it was even more frightening. When she saw that Bella was galloping on towards the horizon instead of turning for home, Irina called to her over the noise of the wind their galloping made, "Don't go so far away, Bella! Please don't!"

But Bella galloped on until she came to the same spot where she had stopped the night before. Again she stood rigid and trembling, with her big eyes fixed on the horizon and her big heart beating faster and faster. Her breath came in sharp snorts.

"Bella! You're frightening me! Bella!"

But Bella seemed to have forgotten that

anyone was riding her at all. She spun round suddenly, then back again. She ran to the left, swung herself round on her hindquarters and ran to the right, then swung round again, and always with her eyes fixed on the horizon. Irina clung on as well as she could, but she slid sideways at each violent turn and only Bella's long mane saved her from falling. She surely would have fallen sooner or later but, just like the night before, Bella suddenly relaxed, breathed normally and turned to gallop for home.

The third night, Irina was almost afraid to go out. But when she looked down from her window and saw Bella waiting patiently by the tree stump, quiet and composed as if nothing had happened, she summoned the courage to go down and mount her.

When they reached the field where they always used to turn for home, Irina said, "Let's go back now, Bella! Please let's go back." But Bella only galloped faster until she reached that same spot and stopped. She trembled so much that Irina started to tremble too, and again she ran back and forth, back and forth, watching the horizon, her ears pricked, snorting sharply.

"What can you hear, Bella, *what*?"

Then she too heard. At first it was a distant, muted rumbling, like a thunderstorm far away. It came closer and closer, and Bella's heart beat faster and louder. Then Irina understood. Hoofbeats. Hundreds and hundreds of hoofbeats, and on the horizon she saw the wild horses streaming along at full gallop, their manes as white as the snow.

Bella threw up her head and neighed, a long, high desperate call that was almost a scream. From far away came an answering call. Bella reared, pawing the air, then she plunged. Irina felt herself thrown into space with the snow and the sky spinning upside down and then the white ground hit her hard and everything turned black and silent.

When she opened her eyes again she felt sick and dizzy and her mouth and ears were full of snow. She got to her feet very slowly, staring at the empty horizon, her ears buzzing in the silence. Then she turned and started walking home. Her feet were bare in the snow but she didn't notice the cold. She knew that one of her hands was hurt badly but she didn't feel the pain, she just knew in her head that it was there. She was very far from home but she felt no fear

of getting lost. She knew that she must go on putting one foot in front of the other but she felt nothing at all. And she never once turned to look back after the wild horses who had taken Bella away.

★ NINE ★

Irina lay very still in her bed. Her face
was white except for a reddish purple
bruise on her forehead. Her right arm
rested outside the quilt with a stiff bandage
round the wrist. She wasn't asleep, her eyes
were wide open. Outside the door of her
bedroom her parents were talking to the
doctor in low voices.

"It's just the shock . . . You'll see that in
a few days . . . no serious injury . . . "

"Sleepwalking . . . she must have . . . we
found her early in the morning on a pile of
straw in the barn . . . "

"Just keep her quiet, and don't worry . . . "

Irina could hear them but she didn't
listen. Inside her head, everything was
empty and silent. The sun was shining
outside the window, and the snow was

melting and dripping from the black boughs of the apple tree. Irina closed her eyes and slept.

After a while, Irina was sent back to school. She was very quiet and well-behaved as usual, but she didn't learn anything. At home, she answered when she was spoken to but if no one spoke to her she was silent. Her parents looked at her and then at each other. They called the doctor. The doctor looked at Irina's eyes and throat and squeezed her neck behind her ears. He said perhaps she was growing too much and gave her some bitter medicine. But Irina wasn't growing. She didn't grow one inch taller and her hair didn't grow one inch longer. The doctor said perhaps she was studying too much. But Irina wasn't studying at all. Every evening she took her books and sat by the window. The black boughs of the apple tree grew buds that opened into tiny leaves of the palest green. Irina watched the leaves unfold and inside her head everything was empty and silent.

The sun grew warmer and the cows were turned out into the pasture. In the evenings, Irina was sent to drive them home to be milked. Afterwards she sat by the open window with her book and watched the

thick white apple blossom ruffled by the
warm breeze that filled her room with its
perfume, and inside her head everything was
empty and silent.

The tree grew small green apples. By the
time they were big and red the air turned
bright and cold. Irina helped her father
pick the apples. They had always picked
the apples together, even when Irina was
so small that she could only stand at the

foot of the tree with the basket. When he remembered how she used to enjoy it and saw how pale and thin she looked now, her father felt sorry for her and said:

"How would you like it if I bought you a little dog? It would be company for you, something to play with."

"No thank you," Irina said, "I don't want a dog."

"But it might cheer you up," her father said. "It would be your very own dog and you could look after it yourself."

"No!" cried Irina, "I don't want one."

"But why?"

"Because it would run away! I'd look after it and love it and then it would run away!" And she scrambled down from the apple tree and went to shut herself in her bedroom.

Soon the apple tree was bare and its branches tapped and rattled at Irina's window, shaken by the first winter wind. Irina sat watching as she had watched through all the other seasons. Inside her head everything was empty and silent, and never once in all that time, even in her deepest most secret thoughts, had she said or thought the name, Bella. Never once had she shed a single tear.

One night, Irina and her parents were having supper in the kitchen. Over the noise of the roaring wood stove a faint moan could be heard in the chimney pots.

"That's a north wind," Irina's father said. "Next thing you know, it'll start snowing. Once the wild horses have gone through you can count on the snow starting, like clockwork."

"Wild horses?" Irina's fork clattered on to her plate. Her face had turned red.

"They come by this way in the spring, as soon as the snow begins to melt," her father said, "but you've never seen them. They pass too far away from here — but don't you remember once that one of them got into the yard and I found hoofprints in the snow? They'll be on their way back to their winter pastures any day now, mark my words, and the minute they've gone it'll start snowing."

Every night, after her father's words, Irina watched by her window. She no longer pretended to read. There was no book in her lap. She sat there rigid and still, her eyes fixed on the horizon, the emptiness in her head beating to one repeating rhythm: "Don't let it snow yet. Don't let it snow yet." Sometimes, exhausted by the waiting, she fell asleep with her forehead against the cold window pane.

Each night she waited and each day the sky grew duller and greyer and heavier. Then, one evening, as she sat there in the twilight, she saw something twirl slowly down between the branches of the apple tree. It was a snowflake. Another fell and another, and as the evening darkened into night the silent snow fell faster and thicker until there was nothing but whirling snowflakes to be seen.

Then the empty silence in Irina's head was flooded with memories of snowy rides and moonlit fields, of a flowing mane and a warm velvety nose that nuzzled her feet, of the thunder of hooves and her fall through the air to the hard cold ground.

"Bella!" It was the first time since that night that she had said Bella's name. Now she wrenched open the window, calling and calling as though her heart would break, "Bella! Bella! Bella!"

The north wind whirled the snowflakes into the room, touching her face with icy kisses, and Irina began to cry in loud broken sobs as she understood at last what the blind man had told her.

"Never say that any creature on this earth is yours, or you'll shed bitter tears."

⋆ TEN ⋆

It was a hard winter that year, hard for the fox who prowled around the locked chicken sheds at night, his ribs showing through his tattered fur. Hard for the small birds who fell frozen from their branches into the snow. Hard, too, for Irina. She had cried until she had no more tears left to shed, and then decided that if she couldn't be happy she could try to be good. She tried to talk more to her mother and keep her company during her long hours of work, and when her father made little jokes to cheer her up she smiled. At school she worked twice as hard as the others to make up for being so behind. But as she walked home alone each afternoon, leaving the shouting and laughter of the village children behind, her heart was as heavy as the grey, snow-burdened sky and it seemed to her that the winter would never end.

But winter always does end, and one night, as Irina slept, the ice on the roof creaked and slid, slid and creaked, until, towards dawn, a great slice of it thundered down into the yard.

Irina opened her eyes. The room was lit with a cold pink light. The sun was only just over the horizon, and the melting snow was reflecting its light. She heard a thin trickle of water in the eaves and another patch of ice dislodged itself and began to slide. Then she heard hooves striking on the icy stones in the yard.

Irina got up and went cautiously to the window, almost afraid to look down. Bella was there. She was standing very still now, watching and listening, her coat and mane reflecting the same cool pink light as the snow. Irina went downstairs. She put her thick coat over her nightdress and pushed her feet into her warm boots. She was trying to keep calm but her heart was thumping loudly.

"Bella . . . "

Bella allowed Irina to stroke her neck but then she broke away and trotted swiftly to the old barn. The broken door was ajar.

Irina started to follow her.

"Bella? Have you come home?"

But before Irina could follow her inside the barn, Bella burst out again, trotted straight towards her, nuzzled her chest, then spun round, jumped the five-barred gate and galloped at a desperate speed towards the horizon.

"Bella! No! Bella!" Irina ran as far as the gate and then stood watching until the galloping form was no longer visible. Bella was gone.

"What's going on? What's all this noise?" Irina's father came out of the kitchen door, half dressed, his hair hanging over his eyes. "Irina!"

Irina turned, but her father was no longer looking at her, he was looking down at the hoofprints in the melting snow, and now he followed them into the barn.

"Well I never . . . Irina! Irina! Come and look!"

Irina looked back once more at the sun rising over the flat, empty fields. Then she went to her father.

He was standing just inside the barn door near the corner where Bella used to live. Irina had never been in there since, and she didn't want to go in there now, but her father insisted. He took her by the shoulders. "Look, Irina!"

The straw she had put down for Bella last year was still there. And standing on the straw was a foal, a tiny perfect replica of Bella.

"It's a female, and a little beauty," said her father quietly. The foal was too weak and exhausted to look up at them. It took all the little energy it had just to stay on its wobbling legs, and one of them, its right hind leg, was lifted slightly off the floor.

"Why, it's lame," her father said, bending to look closer. Got tangled up in some wire . . . " He untwisted the wire carefully. "It'll leave a scar, but it should mend. That's why its mother abandoned it, but why she brought it here is a mystery."

Irina stood where she was, her face hard and angry.

"Why did she leave it? She should have looked after it if it was lame. Why?"

"They have to keep up," her father said. "If they can't keep up, the mothers are forced to leave them by the rest of the herd. She must have had a desperate run to get it here and then catch them up . . . if she did catch them up." He patted the little blonde mane. "Well, I don't think you've much of a chance, little one, unless Irina wants to try giving you some milk from a bottle . . . "

"No! I won't love it! I won't look after it! I won't!"

"Well, please yourself," her father said, "I thought you might like to have a horse that

84

would be your very own."

Irina ran out of the barn and shut herself in her bedroom. When she came down to breakfast her face was still pale and angry. Her father was talking about the foal, and her mother said, "There's the baby's bottle we use when there's a weak calf born, I suppose . . . "

But Irina didn't say anything.

Her father finished his breakfast and put his boots back on. "It'll be dead by the end of the day," he said, and went out.

It wasn't a school day. Irina helped her mother in the house and then in the dairy. They were skimming cream and filling little tubs with it. Irina's mother glanced at the shelf where they kept the baby's bottle for the calves and said, "There's no understanding you, Irina. Last year you spent every hour God sends messing in that barn with a toy horse and now there's that poor creature in there and you won't even look at it . . . "

Irina went on working in silence but her face got paler and paler and her father's words kept repeating themselves in her head: "It'll be dead by the end of the day."

She saw Bella galloping desperately, her

brave heart bursting with the effort to save her foal and her own life, felt Bella nuzzling her chest, trusting her to help . . .

Suddenly the little tub fell from her hand and rolled across the dairy floor. She ran to get the baby's bottle and clutched at her mother's arm. "Some milk for it! Give me some milk for it!"

"We'll take it warm from the cow," her mother said. "That might help."

The foal had given up its struggle to stand on three legs. It was lying on the straw, its eyes almost closed. Irina knelt down beside it and held the teat of the bottle near its lips, but it was too weak to lift its head. She squeezed a few warm drops into its mouth.

"Don't die," she pleaded, "please don't die! I'll look after you and love you. I'll take you out in the meadow where there'll be grass and flowers and a stream to cool your feet. And when you're big and strong enough you'll be free, you'll be your own self. I'll never say you're mine, but please don't die."

She slid her hand beneath the little head and lifted it gently to cradle it against herself. Feeling the warmth, the foal pushed its soft nose against her breast and opened its eyes. It looked dazed, as though wondering where it was, but when Irina pushed the teat near its mouth it began to suck.

★ ELEVEN ★

L oved and cared for by Irina, the foal grew and the lame leg mended. Her pale sandy coat and silvery mane were so exactly like her mother's that, almost without thinking about it, Irina called her Bella. When the last of the snow had melted and the sun warmed the new grass, she led Bella out into the meadow. Bella looked about her at the fresh green world, and her velvet nose twitched at all the scents coming to her on the warm breeze. With a little whinny of happiness, she began to run up and down the meadow, jumping and kicking and sometimes tumbling over on her too-long legs. Then she ran to Irina to nuzzle her.

"Do you like it, Bella? Do you?"

But Bella whirled round and was away

again, galloping round the meadow until she had no breath to gallop any more, and she settled to crop the sweet grass near Irina's feet.

Irina was growing, too. Once she was old enough to please herself, she began to call at the blind man's shop after school sometimes. Now that they understood each other, he was the person she most liked to talk to about Bella and how she was growing tall and beautiful and strong. She called on him so often that he soon learned to recognize her footsteps. One day he lifted his small, mouse-like hand to touch Irina's smiling face and say, "I think you are growing tall and beautiful, too, Irina, just like your Bella." But Irina saw the little smile on his blind face and said, "Bella is God's creature, not mine."

The years passed and Bella grew big and strong enough to carry Irina. One afternoon in autumn, when they had ridden far from home and it was time to turn back, Bella suddenly stopped cropping the grass and lifted her head, her ears pricked.

"What is it, Bella?" Irina asked gently, stroking her neck. But she knew what it was and she slid down from the saddle and stood beside the horse's quivering body, waiting.

She heard the thunder of hooves and then the herd came into view, streaming across the horizon in the autumn mist. "Let her be with them and safe," she thought, and then she looked up at Bella's tense body. She didn't speak to her or try to turn her away, she only watched and waited. Bella's head was thrown high and still, her ears picking up every sound, her nostrils every scent. She was excited and her heartbeat was loud and fast, but her big eyes looked puzzled, as though she were trying to connect the thundering hooves and the scent of the herd with a distant memory, a memory of a world that was all white, a terrible pain, a terrifying flight across the emptiness and a warm nuzzle urging her on. But it was all so long ago that the memory faded with the fading of the hoofbeats. Bella relaxed and lowered her head to go on cropping the grass.

"Let's go home," Irina said, stroking her long smooth neck gently, "it's going to snow."

It was that same day that Irina's mother and father settled an argument that had been going on between them for years. They put on their oldest clothes and rolled up their sleeves and went into the old barn to decide once and for all what were the "Things that might come in useful" and what was "Junk that ought to be thrown out". They were still in there, arguing over part of a rusty old plough, when Irina and Bella came back from their ride.

Perhaps it was all that dusty junk that reminded him of the blind man's shop, or perhaps it was the sound of the horse's hooves coming into the yard, but Irina's father suddenly laughed and said, "Do you remember that Christmas when Irina insisted on having a moth-eaten old toy horse for a present?"

"She was a strange one at that age," her mother said.

"She was, but she turned out all right in the end. I was just wondering, though, whatever happened to that horse."

"I forget," her mother said. "She probably got bored with it in the end and threw it out."